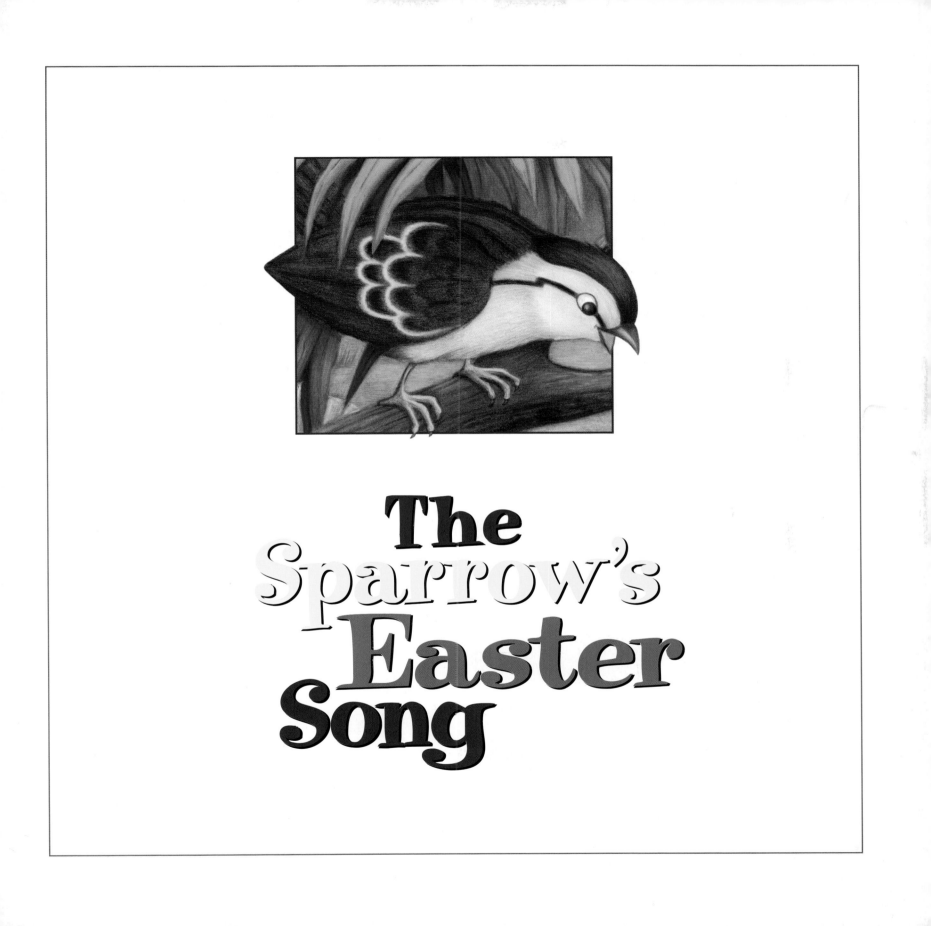

The Sparrow's Easter Song

This book is for

_____

The Sparrow's Easter Song

Written by Michelle Medlock Adams

Illustrated by Marion Eldridge

ideals children's books™
Nashville, Tennessee

ISBN 0-8249-5470-X
Published by Ideals Children's Books
An imprint of Ideals Publications
A division of Guideposts
535 Metroplex Drive, Suite 250
Nashville, Tennessee 37211
www.idealsbooks.com

Text copyright © 2003 by Michelle Medlock Adams
Illustrations copyright © 2003 by Marion Eldridge

Color separations by Precision Color Graphics, Franklin, Wisconsin

Printed and bound in Italy

Library of Congress CIP data on file

10 9 8 7 6 5 4 3 2 1

To My Mother,
Thanks for always being the wind
beneath my wings.
                              —MMA

Sing to the LORD a new song;

sing to the LORD, all the earth.

Declare his glory among the nations,

his marvelous deeds among all peoples.

—Psalm 96:1, 3

"Please hurry, children, hop, hop, hop!"
Instructed Mama Frog.
"The sparrow says he's got big news.
We're meeting at the log."

Soon all the nearby animals
Were heading down the road.
The hare, the deer, the billy goat—
And even Mr. Toad.

"What's going on?" asked Mr. Toad.
"Just what is all the fuss?"
"The sparrow has some news," said Goat,
"Some stuff we should discuss."

Just then, the sparrow flew in sight.

"He's here!" announced the hare.

"Yippee! Yippee!" the lizard shrieked.

"It's time for Bird to share!"

The animals became quite still.

They looked up at the bird.

The chipmunk called, "Hey Sparrow, sir.

Please tell us, what's the word?"

"I've called you here," the sparrow said,

"To tell you what I saw.

A miracle has come to pass!

In fact, I'm still in awe!"

"What miracle?" the donkey asked.

"We really want to know."

"I've seen God's Son," the sparrow said.

"I heard he died," said Doe.

"No, he's alive!" the sparrow shared.

"You see that tomb right there?

He was inside, then he walked out!"

"How can this be?" asked Hare.

"I'm not sure how this came about,"
The sparrow softly spoke.
"But he was dead, now he's alive.
It's true! This is no joke!"

"But I saw what they did to him!"
Declared the chickadee.
"They beat him and they spat on him
And hung him on a tree.

"Then later on that day, he died,"
The chickadee went on.
"And all at once, the sky grew dark.
The sun was simply gone!"

"I do not know what happened next,"
Confessed the chickadee.

"But I *do* know!" the sparrow said.
"'Cause I was here, you see.

"They brought him here," the sparrow shared,
"To rest forevermore.
But he was only dead three days—
Then he walked out the door!

"I was asleep up in the tree—
Before the break of day.
And when I opened up my eyes,
The stone was rolled away!"

"So, that's how he got out," said Toad.
"Tell us, where did he go?"
"I'm not real sure," the sparrow said.
"Is there more news?" asked Doe.

"Oh, yes," the sparrow gave a tweet.
"There's so much more to share.
These women came to see the Christ.
Of course, he wasn't there.

"When they discovered he was gone,
They all were very sad.
But then an angel of the Lord
Had news to make them glad!

"This angel said, 'He isn't here.
He's risen from the dead.
Now go tell everybody else
This thing that I have said.'"

"You saw an angel?" asked the lamb.
"That's cool! Did he see you?"
"I'm not quite sure," the sparrow shared.
"I spread my wings and flew.

"I flew and flew and flew some more,"
The sparrow softly said.
"I flew around Jerusalem.
I had to clear my head."

"That's when I saw him once again—
Jesus, the Christ, God's Son.
He was walking with two men—
Alive as anyone!"

"So what does all this mean?" asked Hare.

"Please tell us," chimed in Goat.

The sparrow thought and then he said,

"It's like the prophets wrote.

"Jesus the Christ was sent to earth

To die upon a tree.

But on the third day he arose

And now mankind is free!"

"That's really great," the lizard said.

"It makes me warm inside.

  And I'm cold-blooded, don't you know?"

   "We know," the tree frogs cried.

"Well that's the news," the sparrow shared.

"This is a special day."

"It really is!" the donkey said.

"It makes me want to bray."

"This news is too great not to share,"
Called out the little squirrel.
"I must go tell the oxen now.
I must go tell the world!"

And so the creatures great and small
Began to spread the word.
They shared the sparrow's awesome news
Till everyone had heard.

But not the sparrow. He stayed home.

He'd played his special part.

And he'd been given such a gift—

A new song in his heart.